The Fred Meyer Foundation

THE LIBRARY FOUNDATION

Serving the People of Multnomah County

Santa Claustrophobia

To Stephen, Marcia, John, Alice, and Max—M.R.

For Mom and Dad—D.C.

Text copyright © 2002 by Mike Reiss.
Illustrations copyright © 2002 by David Catrow.
All rights reserved.
Designed by Debbie Guy-Christiansen

Published by Price Stern Sloan, a division of Penguin Putnam Books for Young Readers,
345 Hudson Street, New York, NY 10014.
Published simultaneously in Canada. Printed in Hong Kong.

Library of Congress Cataloging-in-Publication Data

Reiss, Mike.
   Santa claustrophobia / by Mike Reiss ; illustrated by David Catrow.
   p. cm.
   Summary: Holiday characters ranging from the Easter Bunny to the April Fool try to take
   over Christmas responsibilities so that stressed Saint Nick can take a vacation.
   [1. Santa Claus—Fiction. 2. Christmas—Fiction. 3. Holidays—Fiction. 4. Characters in
   literature—Fiction. 5. Humorous stories. 6. Stories in rhyme.] I. Catrow, David ill. II. Title.
PZ8.3.R277 San 2002
[Fic]—dc21   2002002282

ISBN 0-8431-7756-X   A B C D E F G H I J

Santa Claustrophobia

By Mike Reiss

Illustrated by David Catrow

PSS!

PRICE STERN SLOAN
New York

North of the North Pole and south of the stars,
lies a beautiful village called Stinky Cigars.
The name is so awful that folks pass right by it.
It's a trick that we use to keep our town quiet.

You see, we have got some celebrities here:
The Groundhog, Columbus, and Baby New Year.
Saint Pat and Saint Nicholas fill our saint quota.
(If you want Saint Paul, better check Minnesota.)
There's Uncle Sam, Washington, Lincoln, and Cupid.
That dear April Fool, who's as sweet as he's stupid.
And the Election Day Donkey and Elephant, too!
We're the Beverly Hills of the holiday crew.

There's no place on Earth and there's no place on Mars,
where life is as lovely as Stinky Cigars.
The birds sing the Beatles, the dogs never bite,
the sun shines all day—even sometimes at night.
It's a nice place to work. It's a nice place to grow up.
It's so sweet that sometimes you just want to throw up.

And when someone is having a less-than-jolly day,
they come to see me . . .

My name is Doc Holiday.

The Thanksgiving Turkey has got quite a problem:
He still thinks a Pilgrim is going to gobble him.
Cupid—yes, Cupid—cannot find romance.
He's remarkably shy for a guy with no pants.
Pumpkinhead fears that he's no longer fearful.
The Groundhog comes daily to give me an earful.

Most times the problem is all in their head,
but sometimes their head's in the problem instead.
The April Fool's gotten his head stuck (so far!)
in a jar . . . a guitar . . . and a work by Renoir.
In twelve years of practice and eight years of school,
no one prepared me for poor April Fool.

But I'll never forget the day Santa came in,
a grim-looking grimace replacing his grin.
His cheeks weren't rosy, his eyes weren't twinkly,
his pom-pom was drooping, his red suit was wrinkly.
"Doc," Santa sighed, "I am quitting the business.
I don't have it in me to face one more Christmas."

"There's a nightmare," he said,
"that I have every night:
I climb down a chimney.
It's long and it's tight.
I'm stuck like a cork,
then I start to perspire,
because, down below me,
they've started a fire!
I smell something cooking.
I'm not sure just what.
Is it ham? Is it lamb?
No, I think it's my butt!
I wake up right then
with a terrible scream.
Tell me, Doc, please,
what's the point of my dream?"

"Santa," I told him,
"you're terribly tense.
Christmas is coming.
The pressure's immense.
It's no surprise that the
prospect is sickening:
Chimneys are thinner and
your thighs are thickening.
All those cookies and milk
have gone straight to your rear,
and it's clear you've developed
your own special fear:

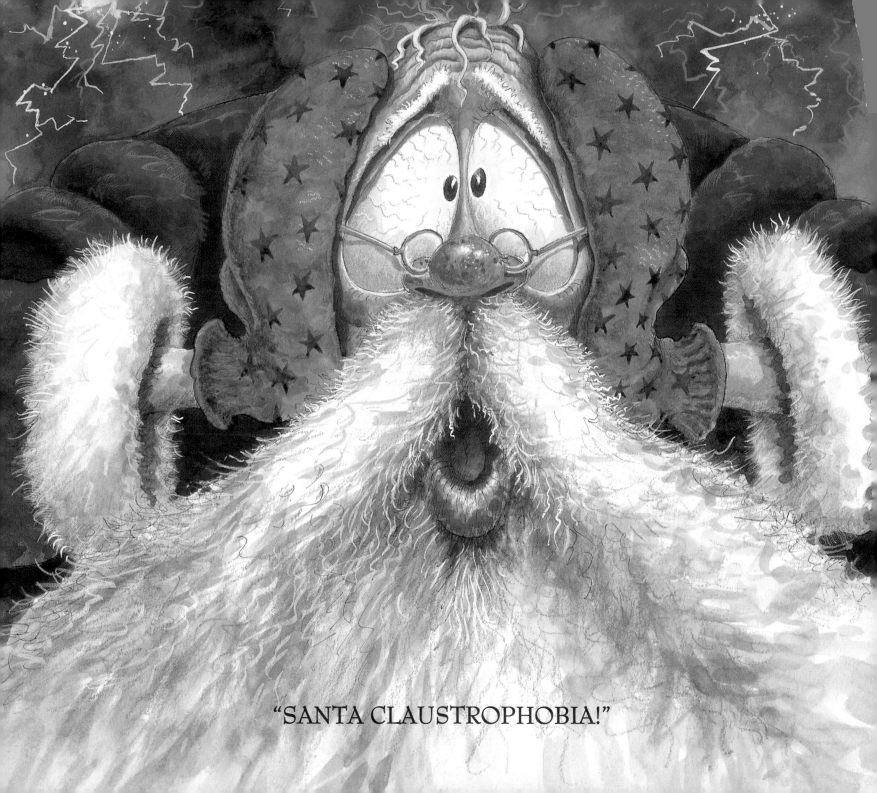

"SANTA CLAUSTROPHOBIA!"

I showed him some inkblots—it wasn't a test.
(My kid broke my pen and my papers got messed.)
But this kept him busy while I made a call.
I soon came back in with a cure for it all.

"Santa," I said,
"it's a bad situation.
You need to relax.
Take a Christmas vacation!"
"I know that I need it."
He choked back a sob.
"But who in the world
will take over my job?"
I said to him, coyly,
"Some folks volunteered."
We went to the window,
and everyone cheered.
There in the snow
stood the holiday stars:
Almost every last person
in Stinky Cigars!
There were even a few
who weren't so famous,
like the Arbor Day Aardvark,
and Labor Day Amos.

"Aloha!" said Santa, as he sailed away
in his shorts and his shades and his Bain de Soleil.
"Folks," I announced, "this is going to be tricky.
So let us unite and win one for St. Nicky!"
Columbus cried, "Bravo!"
Saint Pat said, "Good luck!"
The April Fool said, "Hey, my zipper is stuck."

The Election Day Donkey said, "Who'll take control?"
The Elephant said, "We should just take a poll."
"I vote for me." "Well, I vote for I."
And each time they voted, it came out a tie.
So they voted, and shivered, and sat in the snow.
They may still be at it, as far as I know.

Columbus said he would deliver the toys,
to the good, pretty girls and the pretty good boys.
"I'll sail east to go west, then west to go east.
The voyage should take me three months at the least."
"Uh, Chris," I explained, "you've got one night at best."
"All right," he harrumphed. "I'll go west to go west."

I asked Easter Bunny to gift wrap a truck,
but his paws were too small—he was having no luck.
So he painted and dyed it in purples and pinks.
On an egg, this looks good. On a truck? Well, it stinks.
He did the same thing to the planes and the trains—
The habits of rabbits are burned in their brains.

Cupid was never
afraid to work hard.
He thought every package
should come with a card.
"To Barry Beneski,
Fort Crowder, New Jersey,
We send you our love
and this powder-blue jersey.
Wishing you gumdrops
and rainbows galore . . ."
He wrote on like that
for twelve pages and more.
I asked him just how many
cards he had done.
"Counting that," he said proudly,
"I've got nearly one!"

My plan wasn't working. My plan was ridiculous!
We were about to give up, when this came from Saint Nicholas:

Having great fun in the sun of Aruba
Surfing and snorkeling swimming and scuba
Learned how to limbo, learned the lambada
Ended the night with an eggnog Colada
(Rudolph tried sushi and he's a bit sick)
I miss you, I thank you, I love you
Saint Nick

The holiday gang worked as hard as they could,
and they all did their best (which was not very good).
By the night before Christmas, it all was in crisis—
The Groundhog had eaten the "Naughty & Nice" list.

April Fool was trying to assemble a bike.
Labor Day Amos had gone out on strike.
Six Fathers Time got their beards in a knot.
And Pumpkinhead's head was beginning to rot.

Then Lincoln and Washington started to fight:
"Honest, Abe, can't you do anything right?"
"Hey, I'm on the penny!"
"Well, I'm on the dollar!"
"Stop it, you clowns," I heard Uncle Sam holler.
"Christmas is coming—you're acting like Scrooges!"
They then began fighting just like the Three Stooges.

Through the fighting and tugging,
the smells and the tears,
a voice, soft and warm,
found its way to my ears:
"Um . . . I'm back a day early,
a small change of plan.
I just had to show off
my abs and my tan."
Saint Nick had come back
in the saint nick of time!
He was rested, relaxed—
he looked back in his prime!

"If chimneys are tight, I've got nothing to fear:
I lost twenty pounds—nineteen from my rear!
It's good to know, too, that my friends are so kind.
And that I do more work than this whole town combined!"
Everyone laughed and we helped load his sleigh.
"Thank you all," Santa said. "Thank you, Doc Holiday."

It hadn't been easy. It hadn't been fun.
We'd all pulled together . . . and nothing got done.
But in a way I saved Christmas—it gave me a thrill.
I'd made Santa happy (till he got my bill!).
And I'd just settled down to enjoy my own Yule . . .

When I got a visit from poor April Fool.